EN

"A delicious and delightful story with a large helping of fun and a dash of romance."

~ *Jennifer Beckstrand, award-winning author of the Matchmakers of Huckleberry Hill series*

"I'm ready to pull up a chair in The Sweet Shop, savor a slice of cinnamon bread, and dig into this juicy mystery."

~ Dana Mentink - award-winning author of the Love Unleashed series

"A delightful story you'll not want to put down until you finish it. You will turn each page and wonder what will happen next. Naomi Miller is a talented and wonderful author, and I can't wait to read more of her stories."

~ Molly Morris Jebber, author of *Two Suitors for Anna*

"A sweet, fun and intriguing mystery you can really sink your teeth into."

~ Rachel L Miller - author of the Amish romance series: *Windy Gap Wishes*

CHOCOLATE TRUFFLE MYSTERY

BOOKS BY NAOMI MILLER

Amish Sweet Shop Mystery series

BLUEBERRY CUPCAKE MYSTERY
CHRISTMAS COOKIE MYSTERY
LEMON TART MYSTERY
PUMPKIN PIE MYSTERY
CHOCOLATE TRUFFLE MYSTERY

Adventures of Sophie Kitty

Sophie Finds A Family
Sophie Celebrates Thanksgiving

Sophie's New Home
(coming soon)

AMISH SWEET SHOP MYSTERY

CHOCOLATE TRUFFLE MYSTERY

BY
NAOMI MILLER

Chocolate Truffle Mystery
Copyright © 2018 by Naomi Miller

Chocolate Truffle Mystery / Naomi Miller

ISBN: 978-1948733007   (Paperback)

1. Fiction / Religion & Spirituality / Christian Books &
Bibles / Christian Fiction. 2. Fiction / Mystery, Thriller &
Suspense / Mystery / Cozy.   3. Fiction / Christian Books
& Bibles / Literature & Fiction / Amish & Mennonite.

2018901793

S&G Publishing, Knoxville, TN
www.sgpublish.com

Cover, graphics and formatting by Expresso Designs

First Edition 2018

To God be the Glory...

GLOSSARY

The German/Dutch dialect spoken by the Amish is not a written language. It is solely dependent on the location and origin of each settlement. The spellings below are approximations.

ach = oh

aenti = aunt

allrecht = all right

appeditlich = delicious

bruder/bruders = brother/brothers

buwe/buwes = boy/boys

danki = thank you

Dat = dad

dochder = daughter

du bischt daheem = you're home

Englischer = non-Amish person

freind/freinden = friend/friends

frau = wife

froh = happy

Gott = God

hochmut = pride

in lieb = in love

jah = yes

kaffe = coffee

kinner = children

kumme = come

maedel/maedels = girl/girls

Mamm = mom

naerfich = nervous

nee = no

onkel = uncle

rumschpringe = running around time for youth

schweschder/schweschders = sister/sisters

verrickt = crazy

wunderbaar = wonderful

A NOTE FROM NAOMI MILLER

Chocolate Truffle Mystery was a fun story to create. I enjoyed writing about Mrs. Simpkins' and Mr. O'Neal's experiences, especially how they came to be together. I thought Valentine's Day would be the perfect time to reveal what happened to cause the rift in Lemon Tart Mystery... as well as their adventure during Pumpkin Pie Mystery, when everyone was speculating on why Mr. O'Neal left town unexpectedly. I hope this story wraps up these mysteries in time for a new one that's coming soon!

I would never have imagined, when the Lord called me to write Amish fiction, that I would be writing a continuing saga about the community of Abbott Creek. But when readers asked what would happen next, that's just what I found myself doing—and I love it. I love the characters and situations found in the Amish Sweet Shop Mystery series. I hope that many more stories will be written and that readers will continue to enjoy reading about Katie, Travis, Freida, Hannah, and all the other friends and neighbors found in this series.

This series isn't one that causes goose bumps, along with heart-pounding or stomach-clinching reactions. You can find them everywhere. . . these stories are fun to read, full of love, joy, compassion, forgiveness, and friendship.

As with any work of fiction, I've taken license in some areas of research as a means of creating circumstances necessary to my characters or the plot. I've created fictional characters in a fictional town. Any inaccuracies in the Amish, Mennonite, Irish or English lifestyles portrayed in this book are completely due to fictional license.

God bless you!

~Naomi

And now abideth faith, hope, charity, these three; but the greatest of these is charity.

1 Corinthians 13:13

For Ann

ONE

Monday morning began just like any other Monday—with one exception. Valentine's Day was two days away and there was much to be done if the Sweet Shop was to be ready on time.

Over the past two weeks, Katie Chupp, with the help of her co-worker Gwen Davis, had been baking more and more special treats for the upcoming holiday, most of which were quickly snapped up by the residents of Abbott Creek.

Orders had been coming in for cookies, cakes, and candies. There were almost as many orders as they had prepared for Christmas. Katie was especially thankful that she had a willing—and helpful—assistant.

Danki Gott, for bringing the Davis family to our community. Gwen is such a blessing to me. I don't know what I would have done the past couple of months without her help. Please bless her family with gut health, supply their needs, and keep them safe.

Only a moment or two after Katie had finished her prayer and went back to work, Travis Davis opened the back door and walked in.

"Hiya, Katie-girl. Hey, Gwennie."

"*Gudemariye*, Travis."

"Hey, big brother. I'm almost ready to go."

"Good. You don't want to be late to school," he teased his younger sister. "Katie, I'll come back to pick up the morning deliveries after I drop off Gwen. See ya in a bit."

"*Allrecht.*"

After Travis and Gwen left, Katie went back over the list of supplies she would need to fill the orders for the next few days. Then she double-checked the customer orders that still needed to be filled.

Katie turned at the sound of the swinging double doors, followed by her newest co-worker's voice.

"*Appeditlich* treats for families and friends. I love selling all these delicious treats!" Bella was practically dancing as she pushed through the swinging doors to the kitchen.

Katie smiled at Bella's use of the Pennsylvania Dutch. Many of her plain neighbors would just shake their heads when *Englischers* used their words, but Katie thought it was sweet that Bella was taking the time to listen and learn—and most importantly, using them correctly around Katie.

Bella Stanton had moved to their small community a few days before Thanksgiving. She had applied for a job at the bakery almost immediately and to Katie's delight, was dependable and a hard worker.

"*Gudemariye*, Bella. I hope you had a *gut* weekend. Did you get some rest yesterday?"

"Yes, I actually rested most of the day. For some reason I was more tired than usual."

Katie frowned thoughtfully at Bella's comment. "I still think it would be a *gut* idea for you to make an appointment with a doctor. You think I didn't see how long it took you to get over that stomach bug you had, but I did."

Katie had been meaning to talk to Bella about her health, but had put it off during the holidays. Then in January, Bella had asked for time off. When she returned, she seemed to avoid everyone. Katie was more than a bit worried about her.

"Bella, please. We need to have a chat. Although you keep telling me you are *allrecht,* there have been many times it was all I could do to not send you home to lie down. By Christmas you seemed to feel better, but you still seem to tire so easily. I really think you should see a doctor."

"Well," Bella looked down as she spoke, not meeting Katie's eyes. "I probably should have shared with you that I saw a doctor last month when I visited my parents. Everything is fine. I feel better than I have in a long time." She turned away then suddenly.

"Do you think I should make more coffee? We've already had more customers today than usual." Without waiting for an answer, she went on quickly. "Yes, I'm going to make more coffee." And before Katie could comment, she was heading for the storeroom.

Katie watched the door, waiting for her to emerge while thinking about how, when the bakery had opened only a few short years ago, they had not offered drinks, but so many customers had requested coffee, Mrs. O'Neal had finally made it available, as well as individual bottles of water and juice.

When Bella emerged, she did not give Katie a chance to say anything, moving quickly through the kitchen and then on to the front of the bakery. The double doors swayed silently a moment before coming to rest.

Katie watched for a moment, thinking over what had just happened. She had been worrying for some time now—and it was clear that Bella had no intention of talking with her about those concerns.

When she had *kumme* to work in November, Katie had been grateful for the help, but hesitant about becoming too attached to the young woman—especially since Bella had requested several days off just after the new year. When she had learned that Bella left town, Katie wondered if she would return—or simply go back to wherever she had come from. And Katie had hoped she would return, but resigned herself to losing a *gut* worker.

When she asked Ada Mueller, the woman had simply stated that Bella was off visiting family. Nothing else was said.

Which was another odd thing about the situation. Mrs. Mueller had always been considered the town gossip; she could ferret out details on what was going on with people faster than anyone else.

Mrs. Mueller had been coming into the bakery for years. She would buy a cup of *kaffe* and a danish. Every day she'd sit at the same table for an hour or so. And when her *freinden* came in, they'd stop, sit down and chat awhile.

Katie wasn't certain when it had stopped, but it seemed to be just after Thanksgiving. Most mornings Mrs. Mueller still came by for *kaffe* and a danish, but she rarely sat down at a table unless there were no other customers around. Whenever one of her *freinden* came in, if she was sitting at a table, she would greet them, but after a minute or two, she would leave.

Katie couldn't remember the last time she had heard Mrs. Mueller gossiping about anyone.

I wonder what could have happened to her. . . I do hope no one was unkind to her, although that seems unlikely. She doesn't even chat much with Bella when she comes by, although Bella is still renting a room from her. Perhaps they eat dinner together and that is when they do their chatting.

Still, it seemed strange that Mrs. Mueller had changed so much. Sometimes it seemed like she was avoiding people. *What on earth could have happened to cause such a thing?*

When Bella had returned to Abbott Creek, she'd looked even more troubled than when she had first showed up in town, although she seemed *froh* to be back.

Katie had wanted to ask Bella about her trip, but didn't want to appear nosy. And for a time after her return, Bella seemed aloof and distant, though only a very short time. Since then, she had been happier and more friendly each day.

Dear Gott, please bless Mrs. Mueller and Bella. Keep them both safe. If something has happened to Mrs. Mueller, please protect her and help her to be a blessing to those around her. And whatever Bella's reason for moving here, I pray you will guide her and help me to be a freind to her.

TWO

At the sound of the back door opening, Katie turned, expecting Travis to step through the doorway. Instead, she found herself looking at the sweet face of her boss, Amelia Simpkins.

Nee, it's Mrs. O'Neal—and has been for months. Why can't I think of her as Mrs. O'Neal...

"Good morning, Katie." She practically sang out the words, a sweet smile on her face.

A moment later, Andrew O'Neal followed his wife, quietly closing the door behind them. "And a fine morning to ye, Katie-girl. I'm just dropping off Amelia before heading over to the cafe to check up on Sean."

During the past two years, Mr. O'Neal had teased Mrs. Simpkins repeatedly, addressing her as "Milly" when he knew it aggravated her. Since their surprise marriage in November, only once had Katie heard him refer to his wife as Milly.

Of course, the teasing continued. Mr. O'Neal enjoyed teasing family, friends, and customers. And the people in the community expected no less from him.

Indeed, it would not seem normal if he

stopped his good-natured teasing. It was as much a part of him as breathing, or so it seemed to Katie.

After he had given his bride a kiss, lingering a bit longer than Katie would have expected, he winked at Katie as he waved a goodbye and left.

She turned toward her boss, not a bit surprised to see that Amelia's face was flushed as she stood looking at the doorway. Even though she had only been watching their goodbye, it felt to Katie as if the room was several degrees warmer.

With a small laugh, Amelia turned to Katie. "Whew! That man can really kiss. Who would have thought?"

Katie laughed. She had noticed how often the newlyweds kissed in the kitchen area. And even occasionally when they were in the front room, Andrew would kiss his wife goodbye before leaving. But those were brief —chaste even—unlike what Katie had just witnessed in the kitchen.

She was glad to see her boss so *froh,* but since everything had happened so quickly, Katie felt as if she had missed so much. . . She had been hoping to get her boss to talk about her trip. And since Amelia and Andrew had pretty much kept to themselves after returning from New York, there had been little chance to do so.

When Amelia came to the bakery, she worked in her office for an hour or so, until Andrew came back to persuade her to leave with him, always suggesting a drive or a trip to someplace.

It was wonderful to see them both enjoying each others' company so, but

Katie's romantic heart still wanted to know more about it all—how Mr. O'Neal had found Mrs. Simpkins in New York, how they had made up and decided to get back together— not to mention, why they had made the decision to get married so suddenly.

Freida had only gone on about how terribly romantic it all was, which Katie understood. . . She just wanted to know more about it all as well.

"You seem very *froh*, Mrs. Simpkins— oops. I mean Mrs. O'Neal."

"Oh, my dear. I cannot ever remember being this happy. My marriage to Henry was wonderful, but it was an arranged marriage. We barely knew each other in the beginning. In time I learned to love him. So much so, that I was completely lost when he passed. But as much as I loved Henry, I've never loved, or been loved, or known love, as much as this marriage has brought me." Amelia paused to wipe a tear from her eye.

When she looked back at Katie, the flush on her cheeks was even deeper than before. "I'm sorry. Perhaps I shouldn't have said all of that."

Katie shook her head quickly, intent on reassuring her dear boss. "I am just *froh* that you both worked everything out." She breathed a prayer for help and went on. "I don't mean to pry, but no one really knows what happened last summer."

"Well. . ." Amelia started to answer, but Katie rushed on. "And honestly, I've been wanting to ask how it all worked out. But I wasn't sure if I should ask or even if. . ." She left the words hanging there, worried that she might have gone too far.

Mrs. O'Neal reached out, placing a hand gently over Katie's. "Katie dear, of course you can ask." She shook her head a little and then smiled as she went on. "It's not that we don't want to talk about it. To tell the truth, we have been selfish since we returned. We've stayed away from everyone. We've been enjoying just being together—without anything coming between us."

"That doesn't sound selfish to me. That sounds sensible. I don't think it's selfish to spend time building a life together." Katie smiled, a thoughtful look in her eyes. "I think it is a very *gut* idea. It is just what I would like to do when I marry. . . if I marry."

"If you marry? Well, of course you will marry someday." Mrs. O'Neal shook her finger a little at Katie, and then, a moment later she smiled as if she had a delightful secret. "Why, I fully expect you will be happily married—and perhaps sooner than you think."

"*Nee*, I don't know. Right now it is difficult to think of it all working out. I mean, I would have to be courting." Looking thoughtful, she went on. "And there is no one in our community that I can see myself courting." And before Mrs. O'Neal could speak, she added, "Although my parents speak of it often.

"Why wouldn't it work out? I thought perhaps you were already courting. I mean, it's pretty obvious to everyone how you both feel. We've been wondering when. . . Wait, are you talking about boys in the community or boys in your church?"

"*Buwes* in my church, of course. Wait! Obvious? What. . . who. . . to everyone?" Her cheeks hot with embarrassment, Katie ran towards the back door, hoping to escape. Instead, the door opened and Katie suddenly found herself held tightly in the arms of a man!

* * *

Travis was not expecting Katie to fling herself into his arms when he opened the back door of the bakery, but that's exactly what happened!

Well, of course that couldn't be what she had meant to happen. . . It was pretty obvious that she had rushed to leave at the precise moment Travis opened the back door to walk inside.

Still, it was an unexpected, albeit exciting, moment. Travis couldn't remember the last time he had driven Katie to work. . . or home in his car, or had been alone with her in the kitchen, or anyplace else.

He knew when things began changing between them. It had been almost a year ago when he noticed Katie pulling away, around the time that he found his sister at one of the singings dressed like. . . well, a much older, more experienced female.

Katie had been understanding about it. They had driven her home. Everything had been fine.

Then, the very next day, Katie had seemed different, almost as if she were avoiding him. . . and things had never been the same again.

Travis had had no idea how to fix things. Weeks went by, then months, with no change. Oh, there were times that Katie laughed and talked with him when Freida or Bella was around. But they had lost something—and Travis still had no idea how to get it back.

Today, when Katie bounded towards the doorway, Travis had reached out and grabbed her with both arms, trying to steady her, hoping he wouldn't get knocked aside. Or worse, get knocked to the ground, pulling her with him.

For a moment. . . a long moment. . . Travis allowed himself to hold on to Katie, enjoying the feel of her against him as he hugged her.

All the feelings he had hidden months ago suddenly rushed to the surface. After talking to Jake Yoder last spring, he had even begun to give serious thought to a future with Katie.

Then, after she had begun to avoid him, Travis had decided since she would probably be joining the Amish church soon anyway, there was no chance for a relationship with her.

So why does it feel so good. . . so right. . . to hold her? What is it about Katie that makes her so special? So unforgettable? Maybe this will be a good thing. Maybe we'll get another chance.

Finally, reluctantly, pulling away a little, he looked down at her. She raised her head to look up at him, surprise showing in her eyes. Her face flushed a pretty shade of pink and she blessed him with one of her beautiful smiles.

"Um, Travis? I think you should let me go now."

He smiled back, then winked at her,

before letting go and stepping back.

THREE

The breath left Katie in a sharp whoosh when she collided with a man's chest. And when she looked up and saw that it was Travis holding her, she inhaled sharply. . . and the heat in her cheeks began to spread.

She told herself she should step away, back out of his embrace immediately. Amelia had in essence just said that some people already suspected she had feelings for

Travis. If she was looking at Travis. . . the expression on his face would tell her there was reason to suspect.

But oh it felt *gut* to be wrapped in his strong embrace. The way he held her—so carefully, but tightly at the same time—made her never want to move.

Nee. This cannot be. I cannot leave the church, my family, the community, not like this. We must stop.

When she felt him loosen his grip a little, she struggled against the little voice in her head that told her to lean into his embrace. . . to stop him from letting go.

And then, when he did not, she had to force herself to speak up. It took nearly every ounce of will-power to make herself tell him that he could let her go now.

When he did finally let go, she cleared

her throat, trying to calm the fluttering that his wink set loose in her stomach—and then she spent several seconds straightening her apron and *kapp* before taking a deep breath. After running into Travis. . . literally. . . Katie figured she would need any extra courage she could muster in those few seconds.

If Mrs. O'Neal had not wondered about her feelings for Travis before. . . she certainly would now.

When she turned back toward the kitchen, not only Amelia, but Freida and Bella had joined her and they were all standing there, watching the whole exchange.

"Katie, are you all right?"

And Katie wished her *freind* would not sound quite so. . . excited, but she dare not say anything. She only nodded, hopeful that everyone would think it was only Freida's normal level of over-excitement that had her sounding so.

"What is going on? What did we miss? Bella and I came in to say *gudemariye* to you. Instead, we see you flying toward the back door!" Freida still looked far too excited and Katie tried to find some way to express with her eyes or her tight smile that she should calm down. "Or was it Travis that you were running to?"

And Katie inhaled sharply again, her cheeks were positively aflame now—but, before she could say anything to her mischievous *friend,* Mrs. O'Neal spoke up, rescuing her.

"Katie, before when we were chatting, you mentioned having some questions. Were you referring to my vacation trip?" And Katie was very grateful to her boss for going on as if she had not just made such a spectacle of herself.

"*Jah*. Like you said, you and Mr. O'Neal have pretty much kept to yourselves. We would all sure like to know whatever you want to tell us about your trip. . . and how Mr. O'Neal found you. . . and how you ended up married."

Katie stopped herself when she realized that she was babbling on—and that the heat was crawling up her neck again. Turning this way and that, she tried to think of some reason she could excuse herself. . . if only to hide her bright pink cheeks.

Looking around the kitchen, she latched onto the first thing that came to mind. "But I guess right now I need to get busy with baking. We have lots of orders to fill today."

"Girls, here is what we will do." Mrs. O'Neal said. "Katie, you can work on your baking while we chat. Freida, you come and help Katie, and Bella, you can step inside the kitchen whenever there are no customers to wait on if you want to join us."

She looked back to Katie—and Katie nodded her agreement. At least, if she had something to do with her hands, she might be able to calm her speeding heart.

* * *

Bella walked through the swinging double doors to the front, not knowing what to think.

Wow! When Freida stopped by for a visit, I bet she never expected to find Katie and

Travis together! How long has that been going on, I wonder. They had me completely fooled.

Going around the room, making certain everything was ready for more customers, Bella's thoughts were racing around faster than lightning.

And Travis? How does a relationship work between the Amish and Englischer? I thought that was forbidden. Did Freida know about them? She made a mental note to ask her about it later.

Checking the shelves and display case, Bella sighed with relief. Everything was ready—and Katie had certainly been distracted from asking her any more questions.

When no one came in, she decided it might even be safe to go back into the kitchen. *I hope I haven't missed a lot.*

When she turned to go back into the kitchen, she thought about how wonderful it was to be included. . . especially since Mrs. O'Neal had been away when she was hired. *She doesn't even really know me and she has been ever so nice, including me in everything as if I've always been here. And I've only had time to say hello to her whenever she drops by to. . . well, do whatever it is she does.*

And she had to admit she had been more than a little curious about her new boss's story. *Especially since I heard that she ran away from Mr. O'Neal. And then they show up here, right after I begin working, married!*

So what's the haps with them. . . Then she hurried over to the swinging doors to go back into the kitchen.

Katie's Triple Chocolate Cake

Ingredients:

2 cups all-purpose flour (sifted)

1 tsp salt

½ cup shortening

1 ½ cups sugar

2 large eggs

¼ cup ice water

½ cup cocoa

1 cup hot coffee

1 tsp baking soda

½ cup boiling water

2 oz dark chocolate

Instructions:

1. Sift together the flour and salt. Set aside.

2. Add sugar to shortening until creamy

3. Blend in unbeaten eggs.

4. Combine hot coffee and cocoa. Stir to dissolve cocoa. Add to sugar/shortening mixture.

5. Add dry ingredients, blending

thoroughly.

6. Dissolve soda in water and add to batter.

7. Grease and lightly flour two 8" cake pans.

8. Pour batter into cake pans.

9. Bake in pre-heated oven for 30-35 at 375°.

10. Cakes should be allowed to cool before icing.

11. Shave dark chocolate, using vegetable peeler.

12. After spreading chocolate icing over cake and between layers, cover top of cake with chocolate shavings.

Note. Also makes 30 cupcakes. Bake 18-22 minutes.

FOUR

Katie was using the commercial mixer to make bread when Bella came into the kitchen. Watching the dough carefully, Katie moved to change the setting so the mixer would knead the dough. After this step, Katie always scraped the dough out onto the work counter where she would finish the kneading by hand.

"Don't make us wait any longer, please." Freida had been mixing up ingredients for peanut butter cookies, a favorite of Thomas, her new husband. She teased that she could prepare them blind-folded now, since he asked for them often.

Katie was thankful she didn't try to demonstrate how to make cookies blind-folded. Freida loved to be the center of attention. . . except for the few times she shined a spotlight on somebody else—like Katie.

Four dozen cookies were soon in the oven, filling the kitchen—and the bakery—with a delicious, peanutty aroma.

"All right, Freida. Ask your questions. I'll stay as long as I can today to answer them."

"When you left, we all had the impression you were angry with Mr. O'Neal. So, how did it all happen? Had you made up and we just didn't know? Did you call Mr. O'Neal and ask him to meet you there? Did you really take a cruise or not? And married? When? How? Where?"

"Merciful heavens, Freida! No! Oh no, I did not call Andrew or ask him to meet me." Mrs. O'Neal looked shocked at the very idea.

Katie broke in before anything else could be said. "I am thinking it might be best, Mrs. O'Neal, if you just started at the beginning. This way you can share whatever you like and if there are personal things you'd rather not talk about, then you can just leave them out."

"But Katie, I want to know everything about it!" Freida blurted out the words.

But Katie insisted. There had been far too much embarrassment all around for today already. "*Nee*, Freida. Let Mrs. O'Neal decide what she wants to tell us. Did we ask you personal questions about your honeymoon?"

Flushing a little, Freida looked sheepish. "Okay. I get your point."

"*Allrecht*, Mrs. O'Neal. Please start at the beginning. When you left, you were going to drive to Chicago and ride the train to New

York. . ."

"Right. I bought tickets on the Amtrak. It took an entire day just to get from Chicago to New York City. The train was a new experience for me." She looked a bit flustered talking about the train and Katie wondered if something had happened there, but since she had just told Freida to let Mrs. O'Neal tell the story, she thought it might be best to refrain from interrupting so soon.

Fortunately, the worry in Mrs. O'Neal's voice faded quickly. "I reserved a bedroom compartment on a sleeper car. After I boarded and my bags were safely in my compartment, I freshened up and rested awhile"

She took a moment to pour herself a cup of coffee, and took a sip before going on. "It was such an adventure, eating lunch in the dining car. The food was delicious and the view was magnificent. And when I returned for dinner, I joined three pleasant-looking ladies who were already seated at a large table. I found them to be delightful dinner companions and we chatted awhile afterwards."

Mrs. O'Neal looked absorbed in her thoughts as she recounted them to the girls. After a moment, she gave a quiet laugh.

"The ladies at our table were my age—or a little older. Two of them had taken cruises and they shared bits of advice on how to make the most of a cruise."

"How was your sleeping compartment? Did you sleep well?" Bella asked.

"I'm glad you asked, Bella. I retired a bit early, not knowing what to expect. The bed was comfortable enough; it was the size that took getting used to. The bunks are not quite as wide as a twin-size bed and I'm used to sleeping in a queen-size bed. But once I fell asleep, I didn't wake till morning."

Lifting her cup to her lips, Mrs. O'Neal took several sips of her coffee before picking the story back up. "I decided to take breakfast in my compartment. After checking to see that my bags were ready to go, I sat quietly and made a few notes of what I had learned the night before about the cruise."

A jingle of bells was heard and Bella rushed back through the swinging double doors. There had been a nearly steady stream of customers all morning.

"But Mrs. O'Neal, what happened between you and Mr. O'Neal—even before the trip? I've been dying to know!" Freida spoke up again, her voice full of expectation.

Katie had been kneading the bread dough on the large counter, but she stopped to look at her *freind*.

"Now Freida, you promised to let Mrs. O'Neal tell us what she wants. She might not want to talk about that." Turning back to her dough, she separated it into sections, weighing each one carefully before settling them into loaf pans. Covering the pans with clean cloths, she set them aside to let the dough rise.

"*Ach*, Katie! How can you stand there and say that. . . you know you want to know, too."

"Girls! Please remember we have customers in the next room. If you will calm down a bit Freida, I was getting to that. Perhaps we could give Bella a moment. She might not want to miss out on the story."

"Oh I definitely do not want to miss out. Thanks for waiting for me." Bella moved through the swinging doors just as the bells over the front door sounded again. "What did I miss?"

"Mrs. O'Neal just finished telling about the train ride. I think you heard all of that, but Freida asked again about Mr. O'Neal." Freida was practically jumping up and down by then.

Mrs. O'Neal took a last sip of her coffee and then moved to rinse out her cup. "Well, first, let me go back to the start. . . When I lost my dear Henry, after 30 years of marriage, I had no idea what I would do. I never intended to remarry." She paused a moment, as if reaching for the strength to continue.

"After a time, I felt that I would never move on if I stayed in our home. So I packed a bag and decided to visit a few Amish communities Henry and I had visited in years past. When I reached Abbott Creek, I passed by a house that had always caught my attention—and it was for sale. I just knew it was where I belonged."

Bella was nodding and Katie found herself wondering if the same sort of thing had happened with her—she had settled in Abbott Creek so quickly after all. . . much like Mrs. O'Neal.

"As it happened, Mr. O'Neal moved to the community about six months later. I had just opened the bakery and he would come in and tease me every morning. I never took him seriously—at least not until Christmas before last, when he gave me the most beautiful heirloom brooch that had belonged to his grandmother."

She paused a moment when all three girls squealed. Katie could see how Freida and Bella were moved by the romance of his gesture.

"Then something was said to make me believe he was only looking for something temporary. I was hurt. . . angry. . . and I no longer wanted his attention. I returned his brooch, but he wouldn't leave me alone, so I decided I needed to get away for awhile."

Katie and the others were shocked! Even Freida seemed speechless. They had known something happened, but could not have guessed what.

"As it turns out, I was worrying over nothing. Everything worked out wonderfully." She stopped there when Freida and Bella started giggling. Katie sighed a little as she began rolling out dough for cookies.

Suddenly, Mrs. O'Neal stood, moving away from the table where Katie was working. "Oh dear. Now I need to get to my work. Andrew will be coming to get me and I won't be ready. Can we talk more about it tomorrow?"

"*Ach*, of course." Katie and Freida laughed as they said the words at the same time.

"Freida, I know you want to hear it all today, but I think we had better all get back to our work."

"*Jah, allrecht.*"

FIVE

Andrew O'Neal walked across the street to speak with his nephew Sean, after leaving Amelia at the bakery. As he walked through the cafe, he stopped at each table to speak to customers.

The cafe was busier than it had been all month. Andrew was thankful to be able to say that Sean had done a great job while he had been away with Amelia. No one was more surprised at the results than he.

It was good fortune—especially since Andrew hoped to turn more of the responsibility over to his nephew during the next few months.

There were several good reasons he could think to do so. First, it would leave him free to spend time with his sweet wife whenever he wanted to—and he could always work at the cafe when he wasn't busy. Second, it would give him the chance to spend time doing other things, such as helping out people in the community.

And the best reason was to help his nephew get settled into a good business. Sean had his whole life ahead of him and someday soon he would be thinking of marriage and a family. He would need a business to run.

With a wide smile on his face, Andrew walked into the kitchen, calling out to his nephew as he did so. "Top of the morning to ye, Sean."

"Hey, Uncle! How are the newlyweds?" He asked, with a wink.

"Fine and dandy. Fine and dandy. Hey, you got a few minutes to chat? I've got some things I want to run past you." He poured himself a cup of coffee while he waited for Sean to answer.

"Well, sure. You want to sit here or go upstairs?"

"Let's go upstairs. I'm thinking there will be less of a chance of being interrupted there."

Sean nodded his agreement—and when they met up halfway across the kitchen, he nudged Andrew playfully. "Hey, want to race?"

"Sean, my boy, I'm saving all my energy for someone else." Andrew laughed heartily and then added, "Besides, I'd hate for this old man to show you up." Slapping his nephew on the shoulder, Andrew headed upstairs, with Sean laughing loudly as he followed his uncle.

* * *

Sitting in Andrew's office upstairs, Sean wasn't certain what to expect.

"Is everything all right, Uncle Andrew?" He asked, not entirely certain he wanted to hear the answer.

Andrew only laughed and gave Andrew another clap on the shoulder. "Yes, my boy. Don't you worry about a thing. You've been doing a terrific job for me. But see, that's what I want to discuss with you."

But nerves had Sean worrying over every little thing. Uncle Andrew was the only one in the family who had ever believed in him, given him a chance. He did not want to mess up. And that thought brought to mind his major slip up last summer.

"Okay, but first let me apologize again for my part in your break-up with Amelia. I had no idea that you had fallen in love with her. And how was I to know that you had changed your mind about never re-marrying? Or that Amelia would break things off so quickly without even discussing it with you."

Sean knew the story well. Uncle Andrew had met Bridget O'Conner when he was nine and she was eight. Ten years later, they married. When she had died at thirty-seven,

Andrew was crushed and he had vowed to his family that he would never marry again. How could Sean have known the situation had changed?

"Sean, are you still worrying about what happened? That's all water under the bridge. Everything worked out and we're fine. I couldn't be happier."

Sean let out his breath in relief as Andrew went on. "But that's not why I wanted to talk to you. As a matter of fact, I want to talk to you about your position here."

"My position?" The worry was back, gnawing at him. "Uncle, just tell me what's wrong. Obviously there's a problem. If I'm doing a terrific job, why are we having this private meeting?"

"Because you're doing such a great job. I

discussed the idea with Amelia and she thought it was a perfect idea." Andrew sat back and put his feet up on his desk.

"The plan is for you to take over and run the Irish Blessings Cafe someday. And not after I've grown old and retired, but someday soon. You'll be wanting to settle down when you find a young lass to marry and have a house full of children."

Sean didn't know what to think. . . "Wait. What do you mean when you say take over and run the cafe?"

"I mean to say that I intend for you to take over here. . . if you can see yourself staying in this friendly little community, that is. I mean to help you find yourself a house big enough to hold a wife and children, a place for your family. It's not as if I need the money, after all. I only opened the cafe to have something to do." And with a wink, he added, "And to be close to Milly. I couldn't very well sit in the bakery every day just waiting for the chance to tease her."

Sean sat back in his chair, trying to make sense of everything. Never in a million years had he thought he could ever own the Cafe! "Uncle, I have to be honest with you. When I first started helping out after leaving home and coming to stay with you, I didn't care that much for it." Before Andrew could interrupt, he held up a hand and went on. "Then when you left, and I had no choice but to run it, I think I actually detested it at times! But now. . ." Remembering what his uncle said about taking it over posed another question.

"If you sold it, how much would you want for it? How would I be able to afford it? And what would you do if you sell it to me? You're planning to stay here, aren't you?"

"Of course I'm planning to stay here. My Milly loves it here. . . and although it's not the old country, I've found it to be a home to me."

Sean smiled at the deepening of his uncle's accent. Whenever he spoke of the old country, Sean could hear Andrew's Irish coming through stronger.

"Besides, you know what they say. . . you're never too old to set another goal or to dream a new dream. And that's exactly what I've done. I set a new goal and dreamed a new dream. Now it's your turn. And I've already said I have no intention of selling you the cafe. I want to pass it on to you."

"Uncle, that is a very generous offer. Having this cafe could secure my entire future." He hunted around for something to say. . . some way to thank his uncle, but all that came to mind was panic over the idea of settling down into marriage. "But you know I'm way too young to be thinking of marriage and family."

"No, Sean. I do not think the problem is your age. . . I fear the problem is the age of the young lady. You have found yourself enamored with her, but she is much too young for you."

"Who? Wait? What young lady? There is no one. I get up, come down here to work all day. I fix myself something to eat and take it back upstairs. I eat my dinner, read awhile, and go to bed. Rarely does that change."

Andrew looked skeptical, but he didn't push. "Well, for now that is probably best. Besides, you'll have plenty of time to see her.

In the meantime, give her a few years to grow up. If you're lucky, you'll have the rest of your life to spend together."

SIX

Tuesday morning started out a little more exciting than usual. . .

The bakery had just opened for business. Mrs. Mueller had come in to buy coffee and a danish. She chatted with Bella for a minute before leaving. After she left, a dozen other customers came in to pick up orders for the holiday or to grab a coffee and one of Katie's delicious treats.

Three customers were still waiting when it happened. Bella handed a customer a danish and turned to ring up her purchase.

The next moment, she sank slowly to the floor. . .

When she woke, dazed and a bit confused, she noticed that she was lying on a couch. Looking around, she realized that she was in Mrs. O'Neal's office.

Mr. and Mrs. O'Neal, Katie, and Travis were all gathered around her. And a moment later, Freida walked in to the room.

Bella tried to sit up, but Mrs. O'Neal stopped her. "I think you should lie still for a minute. Perhaps you shouldn't try to get up yet."

* * *

"What happened?" Bella asked.

"My dear, that's just what we're wondering. Apparently you fainted. I know you had a bug for awhile, but you seemed to recover from it. Now this. . ." Mrs. O'Neal asked, while looking down at her newest employee with concern. The poor girl was so delicate, she looked like a strong breeze would topple her. "Do you have any idea why you fainted?"

"Uh. . . no ma'am, not really."

"Do you have any medical issues that I should be aware of?" Mrs. O'Neal watched Bella closely as she questioned her.

Bella's white cheeks suddenly flushed with color.

"Can we speak confidentially, ma'am?"

"Of course we can." Mrs. O'Neal looked

around at the others. "If you will excuse yourselves, please."

* * *

After the others left the room and Mrs. O'Neal had closed the door, she turned back to Bella.

Bella knew she needed to tell her—to tell everyone—about her condition. But she was nervous about sharing her problem with the others, especially not knowing them well enough to know how they would take it, how they would look at her after they knew, how they would treat her. . . think of her.

She could lose her job. She really liked her job. And she was good at it. For another thing, she had made friends with people in the community and she didn't want to lose that. And last, but certainly not least, was her home. Although she was staying with Mrs. Mueller for now, she knew the time would come when she would need to have her own home. And the one thing she knew for sure was that she never wanted to leave Abbott Creek.

No matter what.

When she had visited in January, her parents had made it clear that even if she insisted on staying in Abbott Creek for awhile, they fully expected her to move back home eventually.

And that, she would not. . . could not. . . do.

As far as her present situation was, she knew the time was fast approaching when everyone would know the truth, so she might as well get it over with.

"Maybe you could call Katie and Freida back in. That way, I can tell you all at the same time."

"If that's what you want." Mrs. O'Neal went to the door to call the girls. The moment they walked in and closed the door, Bella looked up at them and quietly spoke the words she had been dreading to say.

"I'm pregnant."

While she gave them all time for her news to sink in, Bella took a deep breath and waited for their questions. She only hoped they would understand.

"Bella, I know this may be a difficult subject to talk about. Thank you for trusting us enough to share your news." Mrs. O'Neal spoke first, her voice calm, quiet, sweet.

"I'm sorry I didn't tell you before today, but the time sort of got away from me. I meant to tell you sooner." Bella spoke quietly, still uncertain. "And I'm sorry I hid it from you when you interviewed me for the job." She turned to Katie then.

Katie nodded, but it was Freida who asked the first questions. "Is there anything else you want to share with us? Is there a father in the picture? Will you be staying in Abbott Creek? What are your plans—if you have any?"

"Oh, I will most definitely be staying." Bella spoke quietly and calmly. "I have already told Mrs. Mueller and she is very graciously allowing me to stay with her as long as I need to."

"And the father?" Mrs. O'Neal asked the question again, though her voice was still quite calm. Obviously she felt the point was important and needed to be answered.

Bella shook her head, but otherwise didn't answer.

"And you saw a doctor last month? Did he say everything was all right, as far as your health and the baby is concerned?" Katie asked then.

"Yes. He confirmed that everything is going well, but he advised me to get regular prenatal care. I'm going to ask one of the midwives in the community to help me."

"Why do you plan to stay here in Abbott Creek?" Freida asked. "Don't you want to be around your family after you have the baby?"

"NO! And please, Mrs. O'Neal, I don't want to lose my job. . . or my home. . . or my new friends here. Please may I stay?"

* * *

Realizing Bella was only getting more upset, Mrs. O'Neal put a stop to the conversation.

"All right, girls. Let's allow Bella to rest a little while. Bella, I'm going to send Freida out to take care of customers while Katie is doing her baking. And I'm going to stay with you. Now, you just lie back, close your eyes, and rest a bit, okay?"

"Yes, ma'am." Bella tried to smile, but couldn't quite make it work. She obediently laid back down.

Mrs. O'Neal covered her with a small, cotton quilt. Turning off the overhead light, she quietly left the room and closed the door behind her.

Bella would need lots of help, starting now.

And she was certain of two things. . . that

Bella would find plenty of help in Abbott Creek—and that she had chosen the right place to live.

* * *

By lunchtime, the news had traveled around the small community that Bella had fainted while waiting on a customer. More and more customers came into the bakery, ostensibly to buy something.

But none left without asking about Bella.

Meanwhile, Katie and Freida were trying to wait on customers, fill the orders, and field questions the best they could. They had been advised to say that Bella was fine and she planned to be back at work tomorrow.

It looked as if Valentine's Day would be the busiest day of the year at the bakery, thanks to

Bella.

Andrew's Banana Bread

Ingredients:

2 cups all-purpose flour (sifted)

¾ cups sugar

½ cup butter, softened

¼ cup milk

1 tsp pure vanilla extract

1 tsp baking soda

½ tsp salt

½ cup walnuts, chopped

2 large eggs

3 ripe bananas, mashed

Instructions:

1. Cream together sugar, butter, and eggs.
2. Add milk and vanilla.
3. Peel bananas and mash to whatever consistency you prefer.
4. Mix flour, baking soda and salt together.
5. Fold in chopped nuts.
6. Grease and lightly flour loaf pan.
7. Pour batter into cake pans.

8. Bake in pre-heated oven for 55-60 minutes at 350°.

9. Cool in the pan for 10 minutes, then set on cooling rack for another 10 minutes before slicing.

SEVEN

Amelia O'Neal had asked her husband earlier to wait until closing to pick her up, so she would be available if the girls needed her —and it was almost closing time before things finally quieted down.

At that point, Amelia called Andrew, asking him to come on over, and to bring sandwiches and chips for everyone.

A few minutes later, when he walked in

to the bakery, he turned and locked the door behind him.

Amelia opened her mouth to argue, but he was insistent. "Now then, I'm locking the door and putting out the "closed" sign and I don't want to hear any argument. You have worked hard and now you need a break." Putting the food stuffs on a table, he motioned for them all to come join him.

"Come on over. I've brought hot sandwiches and chips. Plus I knew you girls would enjoy sodas so I brought several of those, too. Amelia, bring you and me a cup of coffee and Freida, bring over a few delicious treats. Let's eat."

"Should I go and get Bella?" Freida asked, one hand still resting on the swinging doors to the kitchen.

"Or should we just take something back

to her?" Katie looked at both O'Neals and waited.

"She fell asleep some time ago on my little couch in the office. I thought it best to let her rest. What do you think?" Amelia looked to Andrew with a half shrug while both Katie and Freida waited for an answer.

"I think it would do her some good to have a bite—and to get up and around a bit. Freida, would you go and see if she's awake?"

Freida nodded and walked into the kitchen, walking back out less than a minute later with Bella right behind her.

"She was already awake. I promise, I didn't wake her up." Everyone laughed a little at the insistence in Freida's voice.

* * *

In no time at all, the sandwiches and chips were gone. Nibbling on a shortbread cookie, Andrew looked around at the bakery. "I guess you ladies have done all you can today. Tomorrow is Valentine's Day and you'll be plenty busy. Maybe we should call it a day."

"I was hoping you would tell us a little more about your trip—or is this a bad time?" Bella looked hopeful.

"Well, actually this is probably a good time to tell a little more. Where did we leave off?"

"The train ride to New York." Freida replied.

"Ah, yes. New York City is a fascinating place. The next time I visit I will take my husband; he will liven it up considerably."

There was a twinkle of mischief in Amelia's smile—and Mr. O'Neal took his wife's hand in his, kissed it, and then winked at her. "That you can be certain of, love."

"But Mrs. O'Neal, what about New York." Freida was relentless "Did you stay long? Did you do anything interesting?"

"Yes, my dear. I stayed almost a whole week. I had taken an empty suitcase with me and I was determined to fill it before returning. New York has some wonderful shops. And the sites. . ." She sighed a little before going on. "The Statue of Liberty was first on my list. Oh, if I could only convey how I felt when I got my first glimpse of the statue that symbolizes freedom and democracy for America. It's on Liberty Island, you know."

"My dear, as long as I've lived here, I

have never visited New York. Now I canna wait to go, with you by my side, of course."

Squeezing her husband's hand, Amelia's eyes glistened with unshed tears. "I would love that, Andrew. We must plan a trip later in the spring. Perhaps I shouldn't say anything more so we can enjoy the sites together."

"Nae, love. Go ahead and tell your story. We'll make plans to visit all the same places, plus many more, when we make our trip together."

"All right. Well, I purchased a tour. The first place we went was to Times Square, but I can't say I enjoyed it much. It's huge. . . and exciting. . . but also loud and noisy."

Mr. O'Neal laughed at that. "That's my girl." He kissed her hand again. "I could have guessed you wouldn't enjoy it. I'll find a way to make it more exciting to you when we visit."

Mrs. O'Neal smiled at him before going on. "Then we went across the Brooklyn Bridge. It was all well and good, but the only thing I really remember about it was the tour guide mentioning that it's one of the oldest suspension bridges in the United States, and that it connects Manhattan and Brooklyn." She shrugged before going on. "Then we went on to Rockefeller Center. That was very interesting."

She took a breath and closed her eyes for a moment, as if trying to gather her thoughts. "I have to say, the most inspiring part of the trip was when I visited the National 9-11 Memorial Complex." Her eyes filled with unshed tears. "The reflecting pools sit where the Twin Towers stood before. I admit, I didn't even take time to visit the museum, because of the memorial." This time, the tears fell silently. Mr. O'Neal handed his wife a handkerchief. With a wavering smile, she dried her tears, only to find them replaced with more.

Finally she spoke again. "When I visited the memorial, I cried buckets as I stood before it. After that, I went back to my room, ordered room service, and went to bed early. It was all too much, too emotional, too heart-breaking, too awful when I remembered the shock and horror I felt on that terrible day."

She shook herself a little then, smiling. "Well, that was it for me. I had planned to do a little more sightseeing, but instead, I went down to the gift shop, bought several paperback books and a few snacks, then returned to my room."

Still sniffling a bit, Amelia took a deep breath before continuing. "I stayed in my room all the next day, reading, relaxing, pretty much feeling the toil from the traveling, plus the shopping and the tour. It was probably a good thing because the next morning was when I was to board the Royal Princess."

At that point Mr. O'Neal looked over at the girls. "Maybe we should call it a day. I'm going to take my lovely wife home and fix her something to eat. You girls get plenty of rest tonight. You'll need it tomorrow."

* * *

Mrs. O'Neal didn't speak to her husband again until they arrived home. When they pulled into the wide drive, she turned to him with a smile.

"Are ye alright then, love?"

She assured him she was fine and took a deep breath before adding that she wanted to talk to him about Bella. "I've been wanting to talk to you about her for some time now. I just didn't know everything there was to know until now. I wonder dear, if you would join me in prayer for her?" Andrew nodded happily. He was always happy to pray with his dear wife. And after he prayed for Bella, he would thank God—as always—for his dear, sweet Amelia. He felt abundantly blessed to have her for his wife.

God was indeed good. All the time.

"That sounds just fine, Milly, love." And he winked at her as he stepped out of the car. She might not admit it, but he saw the smile in her eyes whenever he called her by the name that had only begun as a way to tease her. That it was now a special thing between the two of them was as unexpected as it was exciting.

He moved around the car to open her door and the two of them walked into the house together.

"Andrew, that little girl needs our help. We can't send her away."

He nodded. "I agree, love. I only wish we knew more about the circumstances. Do ye know anything about the father; who he is, where he is?"

Amelia could only shake her head. "I tried twice, but she wouldn't answer. I have no idea why she wouldn't. . . or couldn't answer the question, but at that point she was getting upset, so I dropped it and had her lie down awhile."

Andrew looked over at his wife then. The sadness in her voice was nearly heartbreaking. "I can't help but wonder about it. She seems determined to stay and Ada Mueller has agreed to let her stay with her."

"Then she will stay. Whatever ye want us to do to help, we'll do, love."

Amelia sighed a little as she continued. "When I called Ada to let her know what was going on so she could watch out for Bella. . . she was not surprised." She looked thoughtful. "That must mean she has known for some time now." She stopped a moment and looked over at Andrew, her expression one of confusion and disbelief. "And you know, that is a mystery all its own. Ada Mueller has been the town gossip since before I moved here. But she took Bella in and never has she said anything about her.

She may have even known about Bella's situation from the very beginning."

"Tis a strange thing indeed, that she never said anything about it to anyone, especially you." Andrew agreed. "And now, Milly, I'm in the mood to cook you something special for dinner. Would you be willing to come chat with me a bit while I cook?"

"Hmm. I suppose I could—if you behave yourself."

"Now, you know I'm always truthful with ye, so I won't be promising to behave myself. On the contrary, I'm hoping to misbehave a little, if you know what I mean."

Laughing, Amelia walked with her husband to the kitchen.

EIGHT

After supper, Katie told her *mamm* that she had something she needed to do at the bakery. After putting on her jacket and gloves, she left the house quickly, giving no one time to question her about what she needed to do at the bakery—at this hour.

Once outside, she took a shortcut and walked across the field towards the road, watching for a familiar car. As she came near the road, she found Travis already waiting for her. "Are you ready?"

"*Jah*. I've been wanting to do it again. The last time we did it, we had so much fun." Buckling her seatbelt, she sat back to enjoy the ride to town.

She wasn't nearly as nervous as she had been the last time. She was actually looking forward to it this time. And she hoped Travis was too.

They could have met right after work, but Katie was afraid someone might catch them. And that would ruin everything. So she had talked Travis into going home for supper, then coming around to her house to pick her up, before sneaking back to the bakery, where they would be alone and no one would be around to stop them.

* * *

After locking the door behind them, Travis went to work, moving several tables nearer the counter. Then he went to the storage room to fetch the ladder.

Katie was opening the large sheet of paper she had made notes on, paying special attention to the designs.

"Are you ready to begin?"

"*Jah*." She said, a little breathless. "Travis, can I tell you a secret? I went to the Bishop this time, to ask if it would be *allrecht* to do it. He said as long as it wasn't too fancy, it would be *allrecht*. I'm glad he agreed. I couldn't do it if he had said *nee*— and I really want to do it."

"Then there's nothing to stop us. Just be

careful, please."

* * *

Excitement filled her. This time she didn't feel guilty at all as she climbed the ladder. . .

Dear Gott, please guide my thoughts and my hands. Allow gut to kumme from it and let it be a blessing to someone. And please Gott, let me not have hochmut, but to be thankful for the blessings you give me.

Beginning at the top, right in the middle, Katie used a light color to stencil the letters "Happy Valentine's" on the large window. Then, climbing down off the ladder, she stenciled the letter "Day".

She moved away from the window, checking the position and finding it nearly perfect. Heading back up the ladder, she then filled the space inside the letters with deep red paint. Once again, she climbed down the ladder and painted the last word.

Below the words, Katie drew what looked like a big ship. Just above it, she added a couple of beautiful, gold wedding bands, locked together.

Once that was done, she moved to one side of the window, stenciling in hearts, flowers, and delicious-looking candies. Choosing several paints, she finished them, before moving to the other side of the window to add more hearts, flowers, and candies.

She carefully painted an intricate pattern of swirls and flourishes all around the design, slowly painting in each tiny curve and curl. When she had finally finished, she stood back to look at the full picture. Travis stood just behind her, so close she could feel the warmth coming from his body as he stood ready to hand her anything she might need to touch up her work.

"It's beautiful Katie. I know you don't want to be prideful, but can I just say that God has truly blessed you with an astonishing gift." His words sent a little shiver through Katie and she quickly closed her mouth, fearful that she might say something wrong and mess up this wonderful moment they were sharing.

It was nearly a minute before she was able to concentrate on the picture in front of them—and when she was finally satisfied that the window was ready, they headed to the kitchen to clean up the brushes and put away the ladder and paints.

Travis had just leaned towards Katie, rubbing at the paint on the brush he was cleaning, when he heard the back door open.

* * *

Mr. and Mrs. O'Neal walked in to the kitchen, looking not at all surprised to find Travis and Katie together.

"I had a suspicion that you two were up to something when Sean encouraged me to take Amelia home early for supper. He knew about this, aye?"

"You told Sean about it?" Katie asked Travis.

"Yeah, and I should have known better. Boy, he can't keep a secret at all." Travis looked disgusted.

"I think it's very sweet of you both to go

to so much trouble." Mrs. O'Neal reached over and took Katie's hand, paying no attention to the paint that would certainly be transferred to her own hand. "We saw the window before pulling around to the back. It's just lovely. So romantic. Everyone in the community is going to love it."

"Mrs. O'Neal, Katie was chatting about your trip last November earlier and I have to admit she's got me intrigued now. Is there any chance you would tell us how you two finally got together. . . and ended up married?" Travis asked as the four of them stood there in the semi-darkness of the kitchen.

"Aye, we'd love to share our adventure with you both, wouldn't we, Amelia? Why don't we go into the front area and sit down at one of the tables. We don't want to keep you out too late, but we'll share a bit of our story."

* * *

"Amelia, you start, then I'll come in at times and fill in the gaps."

"All right, dear." Amelia answered with a smile. "I checked out of the hotel early on Thursday morning and headed for the port where the ship was docked. I got there early and was on the ship in less than an hour. I had to wait awhile to go to my room, but I found a comfortable place to sit and wait." Mrs. O'Neal smiled at her husband. "I can still hardly believe I had no idea you were boarding the same ship. . . maybe even at the very same time I was."

"Aye, well let me cut in here. I had no

idea on Tuesday that Amelia was taking a cruise until I left the bakery and went back to the cafe. The problems between us had started months before, but I had no idea what had happened until that day." Mr. O'Neal took his wife's hand in his and kissed it before going on.

"Sean mentioned something that day about talking to Amelia months before. He had heard me say after my wife died that I would never re-marry, and he repeated it to Amelia. Needless to say, her heart broke at the idea." He smiled over at Amelia before going on. "She must have thought I was just flirting or being deceitful about my intentions. All summer long I was miserable, not knowing what I had done, but knowing something terrible had torn us apart."

Mrs. O'Neal patted his hand, trying to

console him. "But it all worked out, Andrew. God worked it out."

"Aye that He did. And once I knew what the problem was, I knew I had to fix it right away. I didn't want to wait another day." He turned back to face Katie and Travis then. "So I found out that Amelia was taking a cruise, and the details—"

"I still don't know who told you." Amelia broke in. "I asked the girls, but they assured me it wasn't them. How on earth did you find out, Andrew?"

"Milly dear, now please don't ask me to rat out my informer. It was someone who cared deeply for both of us. When I assured them that I could fix our relationship, they told me where to find you. But it was only by God's blessings that I was able to get tickets to fly to New York and onboard the ship." He took her hand in his and gave it a quick kiss —and Mrs. O'Neal swatted playfully at him, but then she smiled and gestured for him to go on.

"Where was I? Hmm. . . I called a travel agent; who worked a miracle with the tickets. Then I packed a bag, called Sean to say I was leaving, and drove straight to the airport. I had a couple of hours to wait, so I logged onto the ship's website to make a few extra arrangements."

"What sort of arrangements?" Katie asked.

"I'll get to that in a moment. When the plane landed it was very early in the morning. I found a cafe that served breakfast, then I took a cab to Tiffany's. I asked him to wait, and afterwards he drove me directly to the ship, with not much time to spare." Andrew winked at his wife before looking back toward Katie.

"All right Katie, now for those arrangements. . . when Amelia went to her cabin, she found a dozen red roses with a note that simply said, 'To the love of my life'." Mrs. O'Neal was nodding as he went on. "The next morning, coffee was delivered to her cabin with another dozen roses. This time the note said, 'Please let me explain'."

Amelia took over then. "Well, you can imagine my surprise when I read the notes. The first one was the biggest surprise. I was wondering who did it? I was certain Andrew didn't know where I was—or so I thought. And, it made me so nervous, I ordered dinner in my room. When I finally left my cabin and went to breakfast, guess who showed up just after I was seated?"

"Mr. O'Neal!" Katie almost shouted.

"Aye, ye're right, Katie-girl. I knew I had to work fast, so I told Amelia what I had learned from Sean—and how wrong he was. My intentions were honorable." He smiled over at his wife. "It took a bit of convincing, but thankfully, she eventually believed me. After breakfast I never left her side, except when she retired for the evening on Friday. But before that, we took a walk in the moonlight and I pulled out the box I had picked up from Tiffany's."

Amelia looked up at her husband then with such a smile, both Travis and Katie looked away for several seconds before Mr. O'Neal took over the story again.

"Well, we can share lots of things we saw during the cruise later, but I guess you'd be wanting to know how Saturday went. It didn't take much to convince the Captain to marry us—and with very few arrangements we stood before him at twilight and exchanged vows. Afterwards I gave up my cabin and joined my lovely wife in hers, which was roomier and had a balcony."

"Andrew, what did you expect? I made my reservation months before you did. You were lucky you had a room at all."

"Aye, Milly. That I was. But the luckiest day ever was the day I met you."

"Sometimes I can't tell if you're being serious or throwing out some of your blarney," Teased his wife.

"Maybe to others, aye, but I'd never throw out blarney to you, my love. And never again will I ever take you for granted."

"And I pray that I never take you for granted, either, Andy." Then she turned to

face the two of them again. "Katie. . . Travis.
. . learn from our mistakes. Don't allow a
misunderstanding to blind your path." Mrs.
O'Neal squeezed her husband's hand again,
then looked at the two young people.

"I know you care for one another. And I
know you have difficult decisions to make.
Don't make choices based on anyone else. Be
certain of what you want—or what you need
—in the future. And when you determine who
and what it is you need most, don't back
down. Don't let anything get in your way. Be
happy."

NINE

On the ride home, both Katie and Travis were quiet. Travis seemed to be lost in his own thoughts, too. Katie wondered if he was thinking of her.

She thought of all the times she had spent with Travis—and the special way he made her feel. He had crept into her heart without her even being aware of it.

When? She didn't remember.

Now it seemed to her that he had always been there. And how was she supposed to make a future without him. Did she even want to try?

The last words Mrs. O'Neal had said to the pair of them before she and Mr. O'Neal had left kept replaying in Katie's head.

Don't make choices based on anyone else. Be certain of what you want—or what you need—in the future.

But how could she do that. She knew her parents—and her church—expected her to attend the instruction classes and then to be baptized. Her parents had been patient, but they had hinted—even spoken—to her about joining the church.

Katie knew that if she chose not to be baptized, they would be hurt. But wasn't that exactly what Mrs. O'Neal had been trying to tell them—not to make a choice based on others, like family. . . or church.

Do I really have a choice? Could I really choose Travis? And if I choose Travis, am I putting him above Gott?

She looked over at Travis. He was driving slower than usual. She kept wondering what he was thinking. *Is it even possible that Gott would be allrecht with me leaving my church and following Travis? I don't even know where Travis attends church. . . if he attends church. . .*

Watching him in the bright moonlight, she allowed herself to wonder what it would be like to have this always. . . She had ridden in buggies before with *buwes* who had driven her home after singings. . . but riding in the car with Travis was so different—more intimate somehow. They were closed in together in the small space, and his hand was usually on the knob of the gearshift between their seats. . . so close to her leg that he could reach out and touch her easily.

He never had, but there was something about knowing that he could if he wanted to that made the drive in his car feel much more romantic than she had ever felt on a buggy ride.

Could she do this for the rest of her life? Could she leave behind the buggies and ride in cars all the time? Could she leave behind the plain life? Could she live in his world all of the time?

She kept watching him as he drove along the narrow country lane, thinking perhaps he would look over at her sometime, but he kept his eyes on the road.

I know you care for one another. Don't let anything get in your way. Be happy.

The words seemed so certain—yet so impossible. There was already much in their way—things they could not ignore. . . mountains that they would have to move. And all they had right now was feeling. . . attraction. There was no relationship. There was nothing to hold them together, no common ground, no ties, nothing but tenuous and fragile maybes.

But dear Gott, I do care for him! I do! I do not understand. Why did you bring him into my life if I cannot choose him? What do you want me to do? Help me please.

She looked over at Travis again. This time, she laid her hand on his arm. When he glanced her way, she gave him a tentative smile. He said nothing. Gathering her courage, she spoke to him. "Travis, say something. Please."

"Well. . . what are you thinking?"

"To be honest with you, I am thinking of what Mrs. O'Neal said before she left. I cannot seem to think of anything else."

"Yeah, me too." He shook his head. "Look, Katie. She means well, but I know what a sacrifice it would be for you to leave your faith. I would never ask that of you."

"You would never. . ." She tried to ignore the hurt that his words stirred within her. He spoke of her faith, but not of his feelings. Could she be wrong about how he felt about her? "Well, but what if my faith was not part of it? What if I were not Amish? What if I was *Englisch*? What difference would that make to you?"

"What difference? What are you talking

about? You are Amish! I can't even. . . no, it wouldn't be right." He shook his head again, quicker, stronger—and Katie wondered if she was imagining that it looked as if he were trying to convince himself, as well as her.

"I know what my family expects. What the church expects. But I keep coming back to what Mrs. O'Neal said. Her words make sense Travis. I cannot. . . I will not ignore them. But none of that matters. . . if you don't care for me the way. . ." She left the words there, worried she had already said too much.

"No, I can't. I just can't do it."

"You can't do what? What can't you do? You can't think of me that way—the way she was talking about? You've never cared? Never wanted me as a girlfriend?"

With a squeal of the brakes, Travis pulled

to the side of the road. Turning the engine off, he shifted and looked at Katie. "What are you thinking, Katie!"

"I am thinking that what she said does not matter because you are not thinking about me the way she—"

"Don't be dense, Katie. You're the only girl I've wanted to be with since I met you." He leaned away from her, looking out the front window—and his jaw was very tight for a moment before he turned back to her and kept going. "I would give anything to be your boyfriend. Anything. I even thought about joining the Amish church, but I don't think I should join just because I want you. A decision like that can't be made because of a person. It should be all about God. That's why you will join the church."

"But what if God is not leading me to join

the church. What if I choose to leave the Amish? What if you are more important to me than being Amish?"

A moment later, Travis pulled Katie close to him as his lips sought hers. Then he kissed her.

Wow!

Katie's mind was a jumble of confusion. Never had she been kissed on the lips. Never had she been kissed by a *buwe!*

Correction—a man.

Happy. Excited. Scared. Thrilled.

Never had she felt such emotions rushing through her. Just as she felt as if the kiss was binding them together so tightly, they would never truly be separated again, he ended the kiss.

As he pulled away, her hand came up to touch her lips. Then she touched his lips, before placing her hand on his chest.

Soft. . . she would never have imagined his lips to be so soft. And hard. . . she could feel his heart pounding beneath her hand.

His eyes met hers, then he kissed her again.

* * *

When he felt her trembling, Travis stopped kissing Katie and pulled her against him in a gentle hug. He stayed that way for less time than he would like, but he knew he had to let her go and back away so they could think. . . talk. . . figure this all out.

When he let go and leaned back, she was watching him, her cheeks so rosy, he could see the flush even in the moonlight. "Katie, are you all right?"

"*Jah*, I am *gut*. What does this mean, Travis?"

"Uh, I'm pretty sure it means I want you to be my girlfriend." He smiled at himself, surprised he could be so cool about what had seemed so impossible just a few minutes ago. "Is that all right? Could we do that? Could that even work out for us?"

"*Jah*. If you want it to, and I want it to, why can't we make it work?"

"Well, yeah, that would be great! I'm just wondering about the Amish-English thing. Are you sure this is what you want? Are you sure we can find a way to make it work out?"

"*Jah, I'm sure.* Travis, are you sure?"

"Of course I'm sure. I lo. . . I wa. . . yes. . . Yes, Katie, I'm sure."

"*Gut*. This is *wunderbaar!*"

"*Gut*. I mean good. I don't know how to

court you, but I know I want to. But we should talk about it tomorrow. For now I guess I should take you home. I don't want your parents to worry." Starting the engine, Travis took Katie's hand and laid it over his on the shift knob, holding her delicate fingers as best he could while driving slowly down the road towards her home.

When he started down the driveway, Katie asked him to stop.

"If it is *allrecht* Travis, I think it would be better if I go in by myself for now. But I am looking forward to talking to you tomorrow."

"How about I pick you up in the morning. We can drive in together. I'll go back to pick up Gwen after I drop you off at work.

"You can just bring Gwen with you when you pick me up, silly."

"Nope. I want a few minutes alone with you, especially without my chatterbox sister. I can't think of a better way to begin the day."

"*Allrecht.* I'll be waiting at the road where we usually meet."

"Goodnight, sweetheart." Travis leaned over and gave her a gentle kiss on the cheek.

She surprised him by turning her head a bit and kissing his cheek before he moved away.

"*Gut* night."

Katie's Red Velvet Cake

Ingredients:

2 ¼ cups all-purpose flour (sifted)

1 tsp salt

½ cup shortening

1 ½ cups sugar

2 oz red food coloring

2 large eggs

1 cup buttermilk

2 tbsp cocoa

1 tsp pure vanilla extract

1 tsp baking soda

1 tbsp vinegar

Instructions:

1. Cream together shortening, sugar and eggs.
2. Mix food coloring and cocoa.
3. Add to wet mixture.
4. Add salt, flour, buttermilk and vanilla.
5. Gently blend in baking soda and vinegar.
6. Grease and lightly flour three 8" cake pans.

7. Pour batter into cake pans.

8. Bake in pre-heated oven for 30 minutes at 350°.

10. Cakes should be allowed to cool before icing.

11. Spreading cream cheese frosting between layers and, if desired, over top of cake.

Note. Also makes 30 cupcakes. Bake 16-20 minutes.

Note. Recipe for frosting included in this book.

Katie's Cream Cheese Frosting

Ingredients:

8 oz cream cheese

8 tbsp unsalted butter

4 cups confectioners' sugar

2 tsp pure vanilla extract

Instructions:

1. Let cream cheese soften to room temperature.

2. And let butter soften to room temperature.

2. Blend cream cheese and butter until smooth.

3. Add pure vanilla and blend well.

3. Stir in confectioners' sugar.

4. Beat until smooth.

Note. In Katie's opinion, this is the best frosting to use for Red Velvet Cakes, Carrot Cakes, and Pumpkin Cakes.

TEN

Travis was looking forward to the party later today. This would be the first Valentine's Day he actually had a reason to celebrate. This year, he would be celebrating the holiday with his girlfriend!

Last night, after he left Katie, he had driven around for a while, thinking about his day. Before he had headed for home, he'd driven to the edge of town—to the only store still open so late—to buy Katie a Valentine's Day card, something that he had never expected to be able to give her.

A sweet card for his sweetheart.

Looking around at all of the hearts and flowers, he had gotten into the spirit of the thing, buying a card for his mom and sister—and candy for his brothers. *Not that they really needed it.* . . but he couldn't help himself. He was just so excited over Katie.

Bobby had already been asleep when he'd gotten home, and while he'd missed getting to talk to his little brother, he was glad to have a chance to hide the gifts he had gotten for everyone.

He decided not to say anything to his family about his and Katie's decision. . . yet. He wanted to make certain Katie wouldn't change her mind. Or more to the point, that her parents or the leaders in her church wouldn't do whatever it took to change her mind.

He'd woken early, said a prayer for everything to be all right and that he and Katie could celebrate the holiday together. Then he had left early so he would have a chance to stop by the only florist in town on his way to Katie's house. Thankfully with the holiday, it was open extra early.

He didn't want to go overboard, but he was still so caught up in the mood. . . in the possibilities. . . he had to talk himself out of several different arrangements before finally settling on something that was special— without being too much—for his new sweetheart. He wanted to do whatever he could to make this day a perfect memory for Katie.

Driving over to pick her up, he thought about how different things were from yesterday. Starting now, his life was heading towards a new direction.

* * *

He was leaning against the car, waiting at the road when he saw Katie walking towards him.

"Happy Valentine's Day, sweetheart." He handed her the card and a single pink rose.

"*Danki*. *Ach*, I didn't get anything for you." She flushed with embarrassment, and he rushed to reassure her.

"It's not as if you had the same chance as I did to stop on my way here. Besides, you being my girlfriend is the only gift I want from you."

When she took the rose and sniffed it sweetly, he leaned toward her. "May I kiss you, Katie?" He asked, hoping she'd say yes, but still not entirely sure of it.

Last night he hadn't asked if he could kiss her; he had acted entirely on impulse. Today he wanted to show her that he was thinking of her feelings.

"*Jah*, I guess so."

"You aren't sure, Katie-girl? I want you to be sure."

"*Nee*, I'm sure."

Rather than lean in more, he reached around her, pulling her gently towards him. Then he bent his head toward her slowly, waiting for her to make the next move.

Almost immediately, she moved nearer until his lips met hers in a gentle kiss.

Their kisses last night had left him

feeling out of control, excited. . . hungry for more. This kiss was sweet, soft, tender and still so much more. It was innocent, but still. . . it was the kiss of a woman—to a man, not two silly teenagers.

When the kiss ended, he gave her a hug, not quite ready to let go yet—and then helped her into the car. Before starting the engine, he took possession of her hand again, amazed at how good it felt just holding her hand in his.

When he parked at the bakery, he rushed to get out first, walking around the car to open her door for her, taking her hand and then walking with her to the building. While she unlocked the door, he stood there, watching her until a light blush crept up her cheeks.

Once inside, he looked around to see that

all was as it should be and then, because he wanted to kiss her again, he walked over to where she was already starting to line ingredients up on the work table.

"I would like to kiss you again, but it's probably better that I leave and pick up Gwen. When we get back, she can be our chaperone."

Katie giggled at that. "You are thinking we need a chaperone?"

"Well, maybe. Maybe not." And he winked at her before adding, "Katie, I've had a couple of girlfriends, but nothing serious. Neither one lasted long. I want this one to last a long time. . . maybe even. . . how does forever sound?" The moment he said it, he wondered if he was rushing things too much.

"Forever sounds *wunderbaar*."

"Well, then how about you give me a

quick kiss and send me on my way. I'll be back before you can miss me."

"*Nee*, I will miss you. But as you say, you'll be back soon. . . with my helper." She giggled again, then leaned towards him and placed a soft, sweet kiss on his lips. He moved towards the back door reluctantly a moment later—and, with a quick wave goodbye, he left.

* * *

An hour later, Mr. O'Neal dropped off his wife at the bakery. He came in with her, bringing flowers and cards for Katie, Freida and Bella. Mrs. O'Neal explained that she planned to stay an hour or so, then walk across to the cafe since she and Andrew were planning a Valentine's Day Celebration for the employees of The Sweet Shop and the Irish Blessings Cafe. Then she reassured them that she planned to return to the bakery—after decorating the cafe–to help out until closing.

They had been reminding customers all week that the bakery would close at three o-clock, two hours earlier than usual. After that, the employees could walk across the street to the Irish Blessings Cafe, where the party would be.

They all knew it would be non-stop action from the time they opened until they closed.

"It's Valentine's Day!" Mrs. O'Neal was more excited than she'd been in years to celebrate the holiday of love.

* * *

Katie had worked extra hard this morning—to get as much as possible done before Travis returned with his *schweschder* —so that she could spend a few minutes talking to him.

Fortunately, Gwen had been distracted by her phone when they arrived and had paid no attention to her brother and co-worker, so Katie and Travis had been able to talk about the party this afternoon and about how they would find time to celebrate on their own afterward. Travis had even snuck in several kisses before he'd been forced to leave, and head to the cafe in time to help out with the breakfast rush.

All morning Katie had worked, making certain orders were ready for customers to pick up, baking treats, and putting special touches on last-minute purchases. They always had extra cakes made up for this holiday because they knew customers would *kumme* in looking for them today.

And they all knew that customers would be lined up on the sidewalk long before the bakery opened. During special holidays, *Englischers* came from as far away as Indiana, Kentucky and Missouri to buy delicious holiday treats. And while there, they would stock up on breads, jams and butters.

The bakery would no doubt sell out of pretty much all the breads and pastries. Cookies and other special Valentine treats would likely sell out before the end of the day and they would have to improvise something for someone. It always seemed that no matter how much they prepared for this holiday, they always sold out of something that someone needed desperately.

Katie wondered if it pleased Mr. O'Neal that his wife's business was going so well or if he worried it would take time away from them. . . especially since he had his own business to worry over. She thought about it as she made up another batch of the heart-shaped cookies she knew Andrew O'Neal liked.

Ever since she and Travis had made the decision to start dating, she had found herself watching those around her and wondering about their relationships.

She watched Mr. and Mrs. O'Neal until he left to go to the cafe. She listened to Freida go on about her plans with her new husband —and she watched Bella as both women gushed about their love.

Bella did not look unhappy for either woman, which surprised Katie, since she would be all alone for the holiday—and with a baby on the way.

Katie wanted to ask her about the father, but between being so busy—and feeling like she barely knew the young woman, the right time simply never presented itself, so Katie let it go.

Instead she laughed with everyone about Mrs. O'Neal sharing about how she teased her husband. . . saying that she would have the most customers today for sure.

ELEVEN

Laughter rang throughout the bakery. "You should have seen them. Levi and Samuel were running as fast as they could to outrun that bull. When they finally made it back to the house, they were covered in mud and slop. Their *mamm* was not amused." Freida was sharing yet another tale about Thomas' younger *bruders* with a customer.

All morning long, the bell had never stopped ringing as customers came and went. Freida, Bella, and Mrs. O'Neal—before she left to help decorate the cafe—took care of them, while Katie stayed in the kitchen.

They truly had a *wunderbaar* system. Whenever a customer came in to pick up an order placed ahead of time, Bella would bring a copy of the order to Katie, who pulled it from the walk-in cooler. Then Bella took it out front where Freida would ring up the order and take the payment. Meanwhile, Bella would take the order of the next customer in line. This routine worked well for the girls and customers left fairly quickly.

* * *

"Katie?" Freida rushed through the swinging doors. "We have a customer who insists that she placed an order—a rather large one—but she doesn't have her receipt and I can't find anything on it."

"*Ach*, is it someone you know? Did you write down what she said she ordered?"

"*Nee*, I don't remember seeing her before. Here's what she supposedly ordered. . . three loaves of pumpkin bread, a triple chocolate cake, and three dozen sugar cookies with red icing."

"I don't recall seeing an order with those items. Do we even have the pumpkin bread?"

"*Jah*, I pulled the three loaves off the shelf and put them under the counter before coming into the kitchen. I don't know if she'll buy them if we can't produce the cake and cookies though."

"For sure, make her understand our policy, that she must produce her receipt in order to pick up an order. There's nothing we can do. There's no time to bake and ice a cake. She can pick one we have made up already and I can make more cookies, but I'll be making sugar cookies with red sprinkles. I don't have time for icing."

"*Allrecht*, I'll go back out and tell her." Freida didn't look happy about it, but she turned away from Katie, taking a deep breath before going back through the swinging doors to the front.

Katie looked after her, suddenly concerned. She realized then, that her *freind* had not looked well lately. Katie hoped it was nothing serious. Perhaps Freida had been working too hard.

* * *

Katie was grateful when Travis came in the back door carrying a sandwich, chips and soda. Frieda and Bella had been able to take short breaks for lunch, but with Mrs. O'Neal gone and Gwen still in school, Katie had assured everyone that she didn't need to stop. Even now she was working on another batch of sugar cookies while she pulled orders for Freida and Bella, who were waiting on customers.

"Mrs. O'Neal told me the others have eaten, but that you didn't take a lunch break, so she had me bring over something you could munch on whenever you have time." He leaned in for a quick kiss, brushing a finger down her nose when he stepped away.

"*Danki*, Travis. That will be very helpful."

Katie wanted to kiss him again, but with her hands covered in dough, it did not seem like a very *gut* idea. At the very least, he would be covered in cookie dough—and everyone would know just what they had been doing.

When Travis smiled at her, she thought he must know just what she had been thinking—and when he leaned in for another quick kiss, she tried to lean into him a little without getting him dirty—and then laughed when he jumped away. . . just as a bowl of flour toppled from the table and splattered everywhere.

Katie looked at the sandwich with a frown. The food looked delicious and while she wanted to stop and eat right this minute, she knew she must stop and clean up her mess instead.

But Travis stopped her. "No Katie. You

finish what you're doing. I've got this." And he planted another quick kiss on her lips before he went off to get the broom. When he came back a moment later, he smiled at her—and she just stood there smiling back.

"Katie. . ." He said her name with a little laugh.

"*Jah?*" She asked, feeling more than a little confused by all of the emotions rushing around inside of her.

"The cookies. . ."

"Cookies?" She said again, still not sure what he was getting at.

"Katie, you need to finish the cookies, sweetheart."

She looked down then, at the dough on her hands and remembered the cookies. . . the spilled flour. . . the kisses. . . and felt heat rush into her cheeks. He was making her feel positively *verrickt.*

Still a bit out of sorts—and over-heated, what with the blush practically taking over her face—Katie went back to the cookies while Travis swept up the flour.

She finished mixing the dough, laid it out and rolled it into a nice flat circle so that she could start cutting out the cookie shapes before Travis spoke again.

"I have to say, it's very flattering to know that I make you so nervous sometimes."

Katie turned, just as he pulled her close and kissed her again. Her hands fluttered in the air a moment as she tried to keep him from brushing against her dough and flour-covered apron, but after a moment, all she could think of was the kiss—and being in his arms.

She would never know if Travis had

heard something—or if he had just chosen to move away then, but he stepped back and only a second passed before Bella walked through the swinging doors.

Panicked, Katie turned back to the table and picked up a cookie cutter, knocking three others down onto the circle of dough at the same time.

Travis stopped sweeping—and Katie thought she might have even heard him laugh. "Katie, you have to stop and eat something. Hunger is making you clumsy." He turned to Bella and added, "I'm right aren't I, Bella?"

Bella cleared her throat before answering —and Katie just knew she had given herself away. "I think you're right Travis. She has been working far too hard today. She certainly needs a break."

Katie looked over at Travis then—and it was all she could do not to laugh at the smile on his face. If Bella had not figured out what they had been up to from Katie's clumsy behavior, that smile was all she would need.

"*Allrecht.* I will take a break. But these cookies need to be cut before the dough hardens."

Bella spoke up then. "You go. There are only two customers out there at the moment and they're just sitting, drinking coffee. I think I can manage cutting out cookies. Take a break, Katie." She turned to Travis then. "Go. Make her eat something and relax for a few minutes."

Travis nodded and took Katie's hand, pulling her toward Mrs. O'Neal's office. When they were both settled on the small couch, he handed her the sandwich with a smile. "I can't stay long, Katie. They're keeping me busy at the cafe today, but I can give you a few more minutes."

He smiled again and kissed her quickly before leaning back and pointing to the plastic box on her lap. "Eat. And I'll catch you up at what's going on over at the cafe while you do. You'll never guess what happened this morning. You know that Andrew hired Ethan Lewis last year to help out and he's been training him to wait on the customers, as well as working in the kitchen. Well, today he hired an older man that was looking for work. His name is Mason Turner. All I know is his name, that he's retired, and that Andrew checked into his background, then hired him to work in the kitchen. Andrew hasn't said anything to me, but I'm hoping this doesn't mean that he's replacing me. I don't want to lose my part time job there, but there may not be anything for me to do now."

"*Ach*, what will you do if that happens?"

"I don't know, but I don't want you to worry about it. I'll find something. . . someplace. "By the way, I heard that you had a bit of trouble with a customer awhile ago."

"*Jah*, we did. She came in to pick up an order, but she didn't have a receipt, and we couldn't find one in the book. And I don't remember seeing anything written out for what she said she ordered."

"So, what did you do?"

"Freida offered to sell her the pumpkin bread and told her I would bake the three dozen sugar cookies if she wanted to come back in an hour, but there was no time for a cake." Katie took a breath before going on with their adventure. "The *'lady'* actually screamed at Freida, saying things I would not repeat to anyone. When the other customers took her to task about her attitude, she left without purchasing anything."

"Oh man Katie, I'm sorry you had to go through that—especially today. And I would love to stay with you, but I need to get back to the cafe."

Since Katie had just taken a bite of sandwich, Travis gave her a quick kiss on the cheek, and before she could swallow, he was gone.

When Travis had gone and Katie finally was able to swallow her bite, she stood and walked back out to the kitchen. Bella was busily arranging the cookie shapes on a long baking sheet. Katie watched, absently eating her sandwich, while Bella finished and rolled the leftover dough together, then rolled it out flat again.

"Katie, everyone has been talking about your beautiful window designs. Freida says you did one a year ago at Christmas. I wish I could have seen it. You have a real talent for it."

Heat rushed to Katie's cheeks at the compliment. She reminded herself that it was *Gott*—not her—who deserved all of the credit and praise before she spoke..

"*Danki*, Bella. It's not something I do often because I don't want to feel *hochmut* about it. I just wanted to do something special for Mr. and Mrs. O'Neal this year."

"*Hochmut?*" Bella asked.

"*Hochmut* means pride. . . or being proud of something. Our people frown on being proud. I would never want to be accused of being prideful over a gift that *Gott* has given to me."

"Oh. I guess that makes sense. Most people I know are filled with pride. They're even proud of stuff they shouldn't be proud of, if you know what I mean."

"Well, I am not certain. But you would know, for sure and for certain."

Katie watched as Bella put the baking sheet in the oven—and a moment later, Bella was heading back toward the swinging doors. "*Danki* for the help Bella. . . and for the break. I needed it."

"Yes, you looked as if you needed a moment to sit and. . . relax." And with a smile, she pushed through the swinging door —just as the bell over the front door sounded.

Katie sighed and went back to work. First, she pulled the pans of finished cookies from the cooling racks. These were the last treats to be done today.

Smiling to herself as she carefully lifted cookies from the pans, Katie was ready when Bella came through the swinging doors with the next order to be picked up.

"*Danki* again Bella. Those cookies were the last ones for today. When they *kumme* out of the oven, the baking is done—and we don't have many more orders waiting to be picked up."

"That is very good news Katie. It's been super busy today. I'm glad we're closing early. I for one, will be glad when the last order has been picked up and we're done."

"Did you rest on your break like Mrs. O'Neal told you to? You don't want to be over-doing it. You need to take better care of yourself now. You have the baby to consider."

"Yes, I did. I don't want to be fainting at work anymore. I promise I'll take care of myself. . . and the baby."

"That is *gut*. You are coming to the party afterwards, right? Mr. and Mrs. O'Neal seem very excited about this party for all their employees."

"Oh yes, I'll be there."

"*Gut*. That is *gut*. And now, I had better get back to work."

"Me, too. Freida will be watching for me to come back."

"Then I will see you at the party, *jah*?"

"*Jah*." Bella giggled. "I mean yes."

TWELVE

Katie was more excited about the Valentine's Day Celebration than she could remember being about anything in a long time! She couldn't wait to see what Mr. and Mrs. O'Neal had planned for them.

It didn't hurt either that this was her very first Valentine's Day with a *buwe freind*. Given how *wunderbaar* their time together had already been today, Katie could hardly wait to see him at the party—and then on the drive home afterward.

The one thing she worried over was once she got home. She planned to break the news to her parents at home tonight about her and Travis. She was more than a little *naerfich* about telling them, but she knew it would make things worse if she put it off.

With a *buwe* from their community she would have waited until things were very serious before she said anything about him. But this was different—dating an *Englischer* was going to be difficult enough. If someone saw her with Travis and told her parents, that would for sure and for certain have them upset with her. She knew it was best to tell them herself, before they heard it from anyone else. Best to start off right. Not to mention, they might be more understanding on this holiday. *Gut thing Mamm and Dat enjoy Valentine's day so.*

* * *

After closing at three o'clock, it took the girls almost an hour to clean and ready the bakery for the next day, but finally they were done and it was time to go.

Travis and Mr. O'Neal walked Katie, Bella, Freida and Mrs. O'Neal across the street to the Irish Blessings Cafe. When they walked into the cafe, Sean, Gwen and Thomas were there waiting for them.

The room was decorated with red, pink and white streamers, and hearts in the same colors hanging down from the ceiling. The big, white ceiling fan in the middle of the room was set on low speed, making some of the hearts twirl round and round. It was simply breathtaking to behold!

Several tables were made up with pretty white tablecloths, and decorative plates, napkins, and cups. There was a long table nearby laden with food.

The large door that led to the kitchen swung open and Ethan and a man Katie had never met before walked towards the table. Katie supposed the strange man was the one that Andrew had hired today. They both put trays down on the table and headed back to the kitchen. Katie glanced back at the trays of food.

One was piled high with small, square, crust-less sandwiches with delicious-looking fillings. Another held assorted bite-size treats stuffed with cheese, shrimp, and crabmeat—just to name a few.

There were two large trays already on the table, one with vegetables and dip, the other with several cheeses and an assortment of crackers. There was also a tureen filled with luscious meatballs floating in a rich, thick sauce.

A smaller table nearby was obviously for the desserts. Besides a red velvet cake—which Katie knew to be a favorite of her boss's—and a triple chocolate cake, there were chocolate-dipped strawberries, plus several varieties of chocolate truffles. There were even a few desserts that didn't come from the bakery, like the homemade banana pudding, which was Travis' favorite, and the fluffy, cloud-like jello salad that Travis must have figured out was Katie's favorite.

* * *

After giving everyone time to fill their plates, Andrew looked around. No one was sitting down to eat. Everyone looked happy and relaxed, walking around, chatting with first one friend, then another. Maybe it was time to share some happy news.

"Ladies and Gentlemen," Andrew waited until he had everyone's attention before going on. "Thomas and Freida asked if they could make an announcement at this time." Freida blushed prettily and Thomas actually looked a bit embarrassed. He whispered something to her and she nodded, then looked around at the others. "Thomas and I want to share some *wunderbaar* news with all of you tonight. Although many people do not speak of it so early, especially to make a special announcement, we want all of you, our *freinden*, to know that I spoke to Mr. and Mrs. O'Neal this afternoon—and today is my last day working at the bakery. . . because we are expecting our first baby!"

* * *

Shouts filled the room and everyone congratulated the expectant parents. Katie rushed over to hug her dear *freind*. This certainly explained what she had seen today. For sure and for certain Freida would be feeling tired.

"Freida! I cannot believe you said nothing to me! I am supposed to be your best friend!" Katie tried to sound indignant, but knew that the big smile on her face would say otherwise.

"*Ach*, it was the hardest secret I have

ever kept. And I knew if I told anyone, especially you, then Mrs. O'Neal would probably say I didn't need to be on my feet working today. So I waited until after work to tell her. But I told her not to say anything, that I wanted to wait until tonight to tell everyone."

"Well, that makes sense I suppose. Anyway, how exciting, Freida, a new *bopli*. *Ach*, I am so excited for you both."

"It is truly a blessing." Freida agreed. "I will miss working with you, but we knew this would happen eventually." Katie wasn't sure what to expect when Freida leaned closer to her. Then she whispered in Katie's ear. "Thomas says Travis came by their farm to speak with his *bruder* Jake for a few minutes today—and that he had some interesting news as well."

"Did he tell Thomas about. . . us?"

"*Jah*, he did!" Freida looked almost more excited than she had before, if that was possible. "And what I want to know is why you didn't tell me? For sure and for certain it cannot be for the same reason I did not tell you about the *bopli*."

Katie might have been embarrassed if she had not remembered that Freida had done the same thing. "Now, Freida, you did the very same thing to me and you know it. You let me—and everyone else in the community— think that you were interested in Timothy Yoder for the longest time."

"*Ach*. You would have to remember that now." She said it playfully, but somehow Katie felt as if her *freind* might still be a little upset with her.

"Freida, please, you have to understand.

We only decided this last night—and today, every time I wanted to tell you, I was afraid to. You may tease me about the way I feel for Travis, but you also know that it will not be easy for us if we decide to be together. My parents, our friends, the church, the community, they will not understand."

Freida took Katie's hands in hers. "Of course I understand, Katie. I also know that *Gott* brought Travis into your life for a reason. If you are meant to be together, you have to believe that *Gott* will help you find a way."

Katie wiped an unexpected tear from her lashes. "Thank you, Freida. You have no idea just how much I needed to hear that. I really should have told you about all of this earlier. Perhaps I would not have spent so much time worrying over nothing."

Freida wrapped her arms around Katie then and squeezed tight. "Let's both promise not to keep things from each other anymore."

Katie smiled as she hugged her *freind* tightly. "That sounds like a very *gut* idea."

* * *

"Andrew, a few of the dishes are almost empty. Perhaps I should take them to the kitchen to refill them so our guests can go back for more whenever they like."

"No, Milly. Let me do it. You stay and enjoy yourself. You worked very hard today and I want you to relax and let me take care of everything."

Andrew gathered up a few dishes and headed in the direction of the kitchen. Pushing through the large, swinging door, he stopped suddenly when he saw his nephew. . . and Gwen Davis. . . in a tight embrace.

And though he'd had no idea that her brother had picked up the remaining trays and followed him to the kitchen, no one could have missed the shout that came from behind him.

"Sean! Gwen! What are you doing!"

Katie's Chocolate Truffles

Ingredients:

    8 oz semisweet baking chocolate

    ½ cup unsweetened cocoa powder

    ½ cup heavy whipping cream

    1 tbsp butter

    1 tsp pure vanilla extract

Instructions:

1. Melt baking chocolate in saucepan over low heat.

2. Stir in butter until melted.

3. Stir in whipping cream and vanilla extract. It should resemble the texture of pudding. If needed, add a few drops of evaporated milk until desired consistency.

4. Refrigerate mixture 15-20 minutes (or until thick enough to shape into balls).

5. Scoop out small balls using a melon baller or spoon.

6. Using gloves, roll around in the palms of your hands.

7. Refrigerate truffles 15-20 minutes until firm.

8. Choose one or more options below to finish.

9. Store in airtight container.

Option 1. Roll truffles in cocoa powder.

Option 2. Roll truffles in chopped nuts.

Option 3. Dip truffles in melted chocolate.

──── EPILOGUE ────

The next morning was colder than usual—
even for February, so Travis waited for Katie
in the car with the motor running. He had
planned to drive on up to the house to wait
for her, but when he'd dropped her off the
night before, she had told him she intended
to tell her parents about them dating so he
thought it might be best to wait a fair

distance from the house. . . especially if she had not had the chance to tell them.

He didn't want to take a chance on getting her in trouble before they even had a chance to give their new relationship a start.

A few minutes later, Katie appeared and Travis climbed out of the car to greet her. He could see right away that things didn't look right, so he opened her door and helped her inside without a word, waiting for her to tell him what was going on when she was ready.

Once he had taken his seat, he turned to her, but she was busily putting on her seatbelt so he pulled out onto the road and drove slowly, trying to give her time.

When several minutes passed and still she'd said nothing, he decided he had better ask her—before they made it all the way into town and had no more time left to talk about it. "Katie, what is it? What has happened?"

"*Ach*, it's just what I feared would happen. Before going to bed, I told my parents that we had decided to court. I knew they would most likely be disappointed, but they were more upset than I expected about my not taking instruction and joining the church."

"What does that mean, Katie?"

Travis waited, but she said nothing else so he pressed on, asking the question he really did not want an answer to. "What are you going to do? Are you changing your mind about us. . . about me?"

It felt like a long time before she finally answered. "To be sure, I'm not at all certain just what to do. I still want to be your girlfriend. Perhaps if we give them time, they will be more accepting of our decision."

"Take all the time you need, Katie-girl. I'm not going anywhere."

RECIPES:

Katie's Triple Chocolate Cake (after Chapter 3)

Andrew's Banana Bread (after Chapter 6)

Katie's Red Velvet Cake (after Chapter 9)

Katie's Cream Cheese Frosting (after Chapter 9)

Katie's Chocolate Truffles (after Chapter 12)

TURN THE PAGE

FOR EXCLUSIVE

BONUS CONTENT

DISCUSSION QUESTIONS

WARNING : SPOILERS AHEAD!

1) There are lots of changes at the bakery. Katie has 2 new co-workers and Freida is only working part time. How will this affect the bakery? How important is it to be a good employee? How important is it to be a good supervisor/boss?

2) Travis and Katie bump into each other. Then Travis is reminded of his feelings for Katie. Should he ask Katie out on a date or let it go because of her church affiliations? How important is it to date someone who worships the same way you do?

3) Mrs. Simpkins came home from her vacation married to Mr. O'Neal Do you think they rushed into marriage? Could this affect their relationship? Do you think they were ready for marriage?

4) Freida and Thomas married in the last story. Why do you think she stopped working full time at the bakery? Should Freida quit working and make a home for Thomas? Do you think marriages would be stronger if women didn't work outside the home? Do you think the

Amish idea of the wife staying home would work for Englischers?

5) Bella is one of Katie's new co-workers. Do you think it's strange that no one knows anything about her? Why would she be so mysterious about her past? Were you surprised to find that she's expecting a baby? What do you think will happen in the next few months? Where is the father? Why do you think she left home?

6) In this story, Sean and his uncle talk about marriage. Do you think Sean is ready for marriage? Do you think his friendship with Gwen is growing towards a dating-type relationship? Is Sean too old to date Gwen? Is Gwen ready to date someone much older? What age is appropriate for dating?

7) In the last story, Katie expected to join the church and marry someone who belonged to the church. Freida thought she should give Travis a chance... Why do you think she changed her mind? Would you change your faith for someone else? Should you?

ACKNOWLEDGMENTS

To God be the glory! HE is THE AUTHOR of my life! God gives me the inspiration for each and every book... books of family, faith, forgiveness, and grace...

When God placed it on my heart to write a light-hearted mystery series, I'm glad I obeyed.

Thanks to my daughter Rachel, who not only designs my covers, memes, posters (well, you get the picture), but is also an amazing author and inspirational speaker. Rachel, I couldn't have done it without you!

A big *THANK YOU* goes out to Pam, my dear friend and founder of S&G Publishing. If not for Pam, I might never have been published!

A huge THANK YOU to my beta readers. They seem to change with each book, but I've never been without them. They work hard and I truly appreciate each and every one of them.

Last, but by no means least, thank you to my awesome readers, who do so much to encourage me and continue make this series a huge success!

ABOUT THE AUTHOR

Naomi Miller mixes up a batch of intrigue, sprinkled with Amish, Mennonite, and English characters, adding a pinch of mystery—and a dash of romance!

Naomi works full time as an author, blogger and inspirational speaker. She is a member of the American Christian Fiction Writers (ACFW) organization.

When she's not working diligently to finish the next novel in her Sweet Shop Mystery series, Naomi tries to make time for attending workshops, writing conferences and other author events. Whenever time permits, Naomi can be found in one of two favorite places—the beach and the mountains.

Naomi's day is spent focusing on her writing, editing, and blogging about her experiences.

Naomi loves traveling with her family, singing inspirational/gospel music, taking a daily walk, and witnessing to others of the amazing grace of Jesus Christ.

AUTHOR LINKS

WEBSITE: https://naomimillerauthor.com

NEWSLETTER SIGN UP: http://eepurl.com/bPdjGn

FACEBOOK:
https://www.facebook.com/NaomiMillerAuthor

TWITTER: https://twitter.com/AuthorNaomi

INSTAGRAM: https://twitter.com/AuthorNaomi

PINTEREST: http://www.pinterest.com/authornaomi

GOODREADS:
https://www.goodreads.com/NaomiMiller

BOOKBUB:
https://www.bookbub.com/authors/naomi-miller

INDIEBOUND: http://bit.ly/1PsB9MR

FICTION FINDER: http://bit.ly/1UOlI5P

ABOUT THE PUBLISHER

Christian Publishing for HIS GLORY

S&G Publishing offers books with messages that honor Jesus Christ to the world! S&G works with Christian authors to bring you the best in "inspirational" fiction and non-fiction.

S&G is proud to publish a variety of Christian fiction genres:

inspirational romance

young reader

young adult

speculative

historical

suspense

Check out our website at

sgpublish.com

MORE FROM

S&G PUBLISHING

AMISH ROMANCE

A Mother for Leah

"Sweet, compelling, and filled with a charming cast of characters who will resonate with readers of all ages."

~ Suzanne Woods Fisher, bestselling author of *The Quieting*

WINDY GAP WISHES
BOOK ONE

Rachel L. Miller

Junior author series

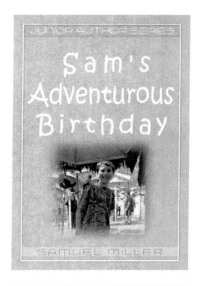

Author encouragement series

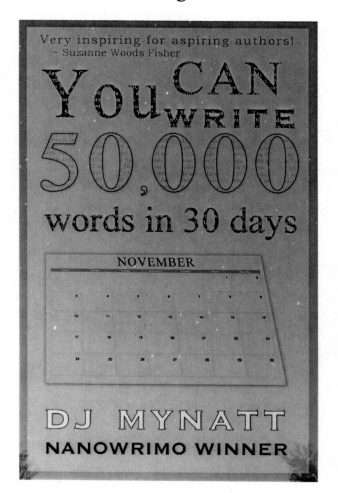